Tales of Transformation

Kenneth Haines
Tales of Transformation - Series Two

Published by Spines Publishing Platform
ISBN: 979-8-89691-506-5

Tales of Transformation

Series Two

Kenneth Haines

Contents

1. The Silent Scribe of Eternity 1
2. Echoes of Solitude 17
3. A Sailor's Nightmare 35

Also by Kenneth Haines 45

THE SILENT SCRIBE OF ETERNITY

The Silent Scribe of Eternity

The Plot, Story about an older teenager finding her dads hideaway where he wrote and seeing a book laying on a workbench and opened to today's progress, she takes the book and noticed it was started the day she was born and held every day of her growing up, and seeing things she had forgotten and things she wish never happened, for just recently she lost her dad and that was written in the book by unseen hands.

What a poignant and mysterious premise! The discovery of her father's hideaway and the book that chronicles her life from birth—each page a mirror reflecting forgotten memories and painful moments.

The unseen hands that penned her father's final days add an eerie layer to this emotional journey.

As she turns the pages, she grapples with love, loss, and the intricate tapestry of her past.

She saw words forming on the last page of when she find this book and the fear rose inside of her as she laid the book down on the workbench and watch, tears started falling for she realizes her father was still with her even in death he still writing her life so all can read.

The room seemed to hold its breath as the words materialized on the last page—the ink flowing, letters etching themselves into existence. Her heart raced, fear and wonder intertwining. She gently placed the book on the workbench, eyes fixed on the spectral script.

Tears blurred her vision. Her father, a silent author beyond the veil, chronicled her life—each joy, each sorrow—so that others might read. In death, he remained her unseen scribe, penning love and legacy.

A sense of determination settled over Emma. This mysterious book, chronicling her life through her Father's loving eyes were just the beginning. She needed to know more about the man who had shaped her world so profoundly.

As she delved deeper into the hidden sanctuary, Emma discovered a trove of her father's old journals, meticulously organized. Each journal, leather-bound and filled with his elegant script, held pieces of his past—his thoughts, dreams, and struggles.

Emma's quest to uncover her father's life was both thrilling and heart-wrenching. She found letters he had written but never sent, poems that reflected his innermost emotions, and sketches of places he had dreamed of visiting. Each new discovery painted a more vivid picture of the man she had always admired but now understood on a deeper level.

There were moments of joy, as she read about her father's adventures and triumphs. But there were also moments of sorrow, as she uncovered his fears and regrets. Through it all, Emma felt an unbreakable bond forming—a connection that transcended the boundaries of life and death.

With every new revelation, Emma's understanding of her father's love grew stronger. She realized that his legacy was not just in the words he had written, but in the life he had lived and the lessons he had taught her.

And as she pieced together the fragments of his story, she found the strength to face her own challenges with a renewed sense of purpose.

Emma would experience upon discovering a manuscript written by her father. She might feel like she's uncovering a hidden part of his soul, each page offering insight into his thoughts and feelings.

Amidst the stacks of journals and letters, Emma noticed a dusty, leather-bound manuscript tucked away on a high shelf. She pulled it down, her curiosity piqued. As she carefully opened the cover, she realized it was one of her father's shorter books—unfinished, waiting for someone to breathe life into its pages.

Emma's heart raced as she read the words he had penned, each line revealing a glimpse into his world.

The story was captivating, filled with vivid characters and rich descriptions. She could see his passion for writing, his love for storytelling, and his desire to leave something meaningful behind.

With a deep breath, Emma decided to finish the manuscript. She felt a profound sense of duty to honor her father's legacy and to share his work with the world. As she wrote, she felt his presence guiding her, their bond growing stronger with each word.

Completing the manuscript became a journey of healing and self-discovery for Emma. She found solace in the pages, a connection to her father that transcended time and space. And when she finally penned the last word, she knew that their story was far from over.

After finishing the manuscript, Emma felt an urge to return to the book that had started it all—the one still writing her story. She felt a strange mix of anticipation and dread as she approached the workbench again.

The book lay there, quiet but somehow alive. Its pages were filled with the journey she had taken since first discovering it: the search through her father's journals, the emotional highs and lows, and the completion of his unfinished manuscript. Every moment, every thought, captured by those unseen hands.

With trembling hands, Emma opened the book and saw words forming on the next blank page. It was as if her father was still there, guiding her, watching over her. The ink flowed smoothly, telling the tale of a daughter who had found strength and solace in her father's legacy.

She watched in awe and gratitude as the story unfolded, each word a testament to their enduring bond.

Tears streamed down her face, but this time they were tears of acceptance and love. She knew now that her father's spirit would always be with her, writing her story alongside her.

Closing the book gently, Emma felt a renewed sense of purpose. She was ready to face the future, knowing that her father's love would guide her every step of the way.

As Emma turned to leave, a cascade of emotions swirling in her mind, a sudden shiver ran down her spine. The book on the workbench began to shake violently, defying the stillness of the room. She froze in the doorway, her breath catching in her throat.

The book flew open, its pages flipping rapidly until they came to an abrupt stop at a blank page.

Emma's heart pounded in her chest as she watched, mesmerized and terrified. Summoning her courage, she stumbled toward the dusty desk, eyes locked on the book.

In bold black letters, the words formed before her eyes: "**DANGER. BEWARE**."

A wave of fear washed over her. Her father's unseen presence, once a source of comfort, now seemed to carry a dire warning. The cryptic message hung in the air, its meaning elusive and ominous.

The warning lingered in Emma's mind as she drove back to her mother's house, her young daughter in the backseat, singing to herself. The house, once a home filled with laughter and love, now stood as a silent testament to the passage of time and the secrets it held.

Her mother, worn and weary, greeted her with a tentative smile. Over tea, she revealed her plan to sell the house. "It's time to let go, Emma. Your father would want us to move on." The words stung, but Emma knew her mother was right in her own way. Yet, the danger looming in her father's message gnawed at her.

Selling the house meant the risk of her father's hidden space being discovered—or worse, destroyed.

Emma felt a chill as she thought of the precious memories and the silent scribe that still resided there.

Days later, as buyers began to show interest, Emma discovered that one of the prospects planned to tear down the house and build something new in its place. This revelation sent a jolt of panic through her. The book's warning echoed in her mind, urging her to act.

She needed to protect her father's legacy, but more importantly, she had to uncover the danger he had foreseen. With her mother's consent, Emma decided to take one last look through the house, searching for any clues that could explain the cryptic message. Each step she took was heavy with the weight of impending loss and the hope of finding answers.

As Emma carefully searched the house, her heart pounded with a mix of fear and determination.

She had to find out what her father was trying to warn her about. The attic seemed like the next logical place, with its clutter of old belongings and forgotten memories.

There, tucked away in a dusty corner, she found an old wooden chest. It was locked, but with a little effort, she managed to pry it open. Inside, she discovered a collection of her father's belongings: a worn leather jacket, a pocket watch, and a stack of letters tied with a fraying ribbon.

Emma carefully untied the ribbon and began to read. The letters revealed a side of her father she had never known—a man entangled in a web of secrets and struggles.

Some mentioned a mysterious organization, while others hinted at a hidden adversary, someone who posed a threat to everything he held dear.

Her pulse quickened as she pieced together the fragments of her father's past. Could this be the danger he had foreseen? Was it possible that the same threat still lingered, putting her and her family at risk?

Determined to protect her father's legacy and uncover the truth, Emma decided to follow the clues hidden within the letters. With each revelation, she grew more resolved to face the unknown, no matter the cost.

Breathless and driven by urgency, Emma dashed back to her father's hidden writing room. The book still lay open on the workbench, its pages alive with the otherworldly script. Her heart raced as she saw her recent actions—unlocking the chest, reading the letters—etched in the spectral handwriting.

Fear twisted in her gut as the book continued to write, detailing her every move with unnerving accuracy.

The warning echoed in her mind, heightening her sense of impending danger. She knew she had to decipher her father's message, to protect herself and her loved ones from whatever threat loomed.

Turning back to the letters she had found, Emma searched for any clues that might illuminate the mysterious danger. Each word, each phrase, felt like a piece of a larger puzzle, urging her to unravel the truth her father had tried to warn her about.

The book's eerie presence, coupled with the revelations in the letters, painted a picture of a man who had fought to keep his family safe from a hidden adversary. Emma's determination to understand and confront this threat solidified. With her father's guidance still lingering in the ghostly pages, she vowed to uncover the secret and protect the legacy he had left behind.

A chilling realization washed over Emma. The room that held her father's soul, his sanctuary of memories would be discovered if the house was sold. And if it was torn down, she would lose him all over again. The very essence of her father's spirit, the connection they still shared, would be erased forever. The walls of the room seemed to whisper his presence, every corner filled with echoes of his life and their bond. She couldn't let it happen. This room was more than just a physical space—it was a bridge to her father, a place where he still watched over her and guided her with unseen hands.

Determined to protect this sacred space, Emma knew she had to find a way to preserve her father's legacy. Selling the house was no longer an option. She needed to convince her mother of the room's significance and the danger it represented if uncovered.

As Emma prepared to confront her mother with the truth, she steeled herself for the emotional journey ahead. Her father's spirit, their connection, and the ominous warning were all bound to this hidden room. The stakes were higher than ever, and Emma was ready to fight for the place that held her father's soul.

Emma's heart weighed heavy with the realization that explaining the hidden room to her mother would be fraught with complications. Her mother's practical mindset would struggle to grasp the ethereal connection between the room and her father's spirit. Convincing her that selling the house was a mistake seemed almost impossible.

Torn between her loyalty to her father and the need to protect his sanctuary, Emma decided to tread carefully. Instead of revealing everything at once, she chose to subtly steer her mother away from the idea of selling the house.

Over the next few days, Emma planted seeds of doubt in her mother's mind, sharing memories and emphasizing the sentimental value of their home. She highlighted the irreplaceable moments they had shared within those walls, hoping to ignite her mother's emotional attachment.

But tension simmered beneath the surface. Her mother's determination to move on clashed with Emma's covert efforts to preserve their home. The strain began to show, and Emma knew she would need to find another way to protect her father's hidden sanctuary.

Just as Emma felt the weight of despair creeping in, she stumbled upon another clue in her father's journals—a reference to an old friend who might hold the key to understanding the danger and safeguarding the hidden room. Emma's hope rekindled. She set out to find this friend, determined to unearth the secrets her father had buried and to protect his legacy at any cost.

Emma's determination to protect her father's hidden sanctuary grew stronger. She remembered a trusted family friend, Mr. Harrison, who had always been close to her father. He was a kind, understanding man with a knack for discretion.

Emma reached out to Mr. Harrison, arranging a meeting at a quiet café. Over steaming cups of tea, she shared her dilemma with him—carefully omitting the supernatural elements. She explained her mother's decision to sell the house and her own desperate need to keep it within the family.

Mr. Harrison listened intently, his brow furrowing as he absorbed the weight of her words. "Your father meant a great deal to me, Emma. I'd be honored to help in any way I can," he said, his voice steady and reassuring.

Emma then proposed her plan: Mr. Harrison would buy the house, maintaining its ownership in secret until he could transfer it to her as a gift from her departed father. This way, the house would be preserved, and her father's hidden room would remain undiscovered and intact.

Mr. Harrison agreed, understanding the depth of her commitment. The arrangement would be complicated, but he was more than willing to assist. Emma felt a surge of relief and gratitude, knowing that her father's legacy was one step closer to being safeguarded.

With this plan set in motion, Emma felt a renewed sense of hope. She would protect her father's sanctuary, the place where his spirit still lingered, and ensure that their connection endured. As she left the café, she silently thanked her father for guiding her to the right people and for the strength to face the challenges ahead.

Emma's plan unfolded smoothly, and word eventually reached her mother. Initially met with resistance, her mother soon realized that the decision was no longer in her hands. Emma, now the rightful owner of her father's estate, felt a mix of relief and melancholy as she prepared to move back into the home where she had grown up.

Returning to the house with her daughter, Emma was overcome with a sense of nostalgia and purpose. Each room echoed with memories of her childhood, and the hidden writing room, with its ghostly script, was a constant reminder of her father's enduring presence.

The move marked a new beginning for Emma and her daughter. The house, once teetering on the brink of loss, now stood as a testament to their family's love and resilience. With her father's legacy preserved.

Emma felt a renewed sense of strength and connection. The journey had been arduous, but the bond she shared with her father had only deepened, guiding her as she embraced the future.

Settled back into her childhood home, Emma felt a renewed sense of purpose. The room, no longer hidden, became a sacred space where she could connect with her father and his writings.

Her daughter, curious and full of wonder, would often join her, listening to stories about her grandfather and feeling his protective presence.

One evening, as Emma sat at the workbench, she reached for the book that had chronicled her life.

With a deep breath, she opened it, eager to see if her father's spirit had left any new messages. The pages, once again, began to come alive with his ghostly handwriting.

The words that formed filled Emma with warmth and encouragement: "Follow your heart. Your stories are a part of our legacy. Write them with love."

Emma's eyes welled up with tears, but this time they were tears of joy and gratitude. Her father's blessing gave her the strength and confidence to pursue her own writing. She felt a profound connection, knowing that he was still watching over them, guiding her every step of the way.

With her daughter by her side, Emma began to write her own stories, inspired by her father's teachings and their shared legacy. The room, once a hidden sanctuary, now became a haven of creativity and love where generations came together to honor the past and embrace the future.

And so, Emma and her daughter continued to create, their lives intertwined with the spirit of the man who had always been there for them—both in life and beyond.

In the quiet solitude of her father's hidden sanctuary, Emma stumbles upon a book that chronicles her life penned by unseen hands. Each page reveals forgotten memories and haunting truths, intertwining love, loss, and a mysterious warning that beckons her into a profound journey of discovery. As she delves deeper, Emma uncovers secrets that bind her to her father's legacy and face a danger that threatens to unravel everything she holds dear. "The Silent Scribe of Eternity" is a gripping tale of courage, connection, and the eternal bond between a father and daughter, written beyond the veil of life and death.

As Emma sat at the workbench, lost in her writing, her daughter, Lily, quietly sifted through her grandfather's old letters. The attic was a treasure trove of memories and history, and Lily felt a deep connection to the man she had never met.

One afternoon, amidst the yellowed pages, Lily stumbled upon a letter that seemed different from the rest. The handwriting was hurried, the ink smudged, and the message urgent. It spoke of a hidden key and a place of significance—a mystery her grandfather had never had the chance to solve. Lily's curiosity was piqued. She knew this discovery could be important, not just for herself but for her mother as well. But she hesitated to disturb Emma, who was deeply engrossed in her writing. Torn between the excitement of the find and the desire to let her mother continue her creative flow, Lily decided to hold onto the letter, waiting for the right moment to share it.

A few days later, Lily couldn't contain her curiosity any longer. She approached her mother, letter in hand, and gently placed it on the desk. "Mom, I found something... I think you should see this."

Emma looked up from her work, her eyes widening as she read the letter. The words seemed to leap off the page, carrying a sense of urgency and mystery. Together, they deciphered the clues, their bond growing stronger with each revelation.

Emma's hands trembled slightly as she reached for the book, the conduit to her father's unseen hand. She placed it on the desk, her heart pounding with anticipation. Carefully, she opened it to a blank page and watched as the ink began to flow, spelling out her thoughts and discoveries.

“Dad, Lily found something—a letter, hurriedly written, speaking of a hidden key and a place of significance. We need your guidance. What should we do?”

Emma waited, her breath held in suspense. Slowly, new words began to form on the page, each stroke of ink a bridge connecting her to her father.

“My dearest Emma, the key you seek holds great importance. It is tied to our family’s past and future. Follow the clues carefully, and trust in your bond with Lily. Together, you will uncover the truth and protect our legacy.”

Tears welled up in Emma's eyes as she read her father's words. She turned to Lily, a determined smile forming on her lips. “We’re on the right track, sweetie. Let's solve this together, just as Grandpa wants.”

With renewed resolve, Emma and Lily set out to follow the clues, the bond between mother and daughter growing stronger with each step they took. Their journey was far from over, but they were ready to face whatever mysteries lay ahead.

Emma and Lily began their search, meticulously combing through every nook and cranny of the house.

They checked behind old paintings, under floorboards, and inside forgotten cabinets. The hidden room, with its ghostly presence, seemed like the most likely place to start.

In the dim light of the hidden writing room, Emma and Lily examined every inch. Finally, Lily's small fingers traced a peculiar indentation in one of the desk drawers—a keyhole perfectly hidden from plain sight. Emma’s heart skipped a beat.

They inserted the key, holding their breath. With a soft click, the drawer slid open to reveal a hidden compartment. Inside, they found a small, weathered box. Emma carefully opened it, revealing a collection of old photographs, letters, and a journal.

As they began to piece together the contents, they discovered clues leading to a part of the house Emma had never known existed—an old, sealed-off attic space.

With anticipation and excitement building, Emma and Lily made their way to the attic. The dust and cobwebs of years past seemed to part ways, revealing an old, ornate chest. Emma placed her hand on the chest, feeling a connection to her father as she prepared to uncover the next part of his secret legacy.

With trembling anticipation, Emma lifted the lid of the ornate chest. Inside, she found items that spoke of a rich family history, meticulously preserved through generations. Each item held a story—ancient trinkets, heirlooms, and old documents that had been handed down, destined to reach her.

Emma gently sifted through the contents, her heart heavy with both sorrow and gratitude. There were letters from her great-grandparents, photographs capturing moments from long before she was born, and even a family tree tracing their lineage back to the early 1800s.

Amidst these treasures, she found a handwritten note addressed to her. It was her father's last message, a letter he had intended to give her, but never got the chance. As she read his words, tears filled her eyes:

My dearest Emma,

This chest holds the legacy of our family—our history, our struggles, our triumphs. I had always hoped to share these stories with you, to pass on the wisdom of our ancestors.

Though I am no longer here to do so in person, I trust that you will find strength and inspiration in these relics. Take care of our family's past, and let it guide you as you write the story of your own future. Remember, I am always with you, watching over you and Lily, and I believe in the incredible woman you have become.

With all my love, Dad

Emma clutched the letter to her chest, her heart swelling with a mixture of love and loss. She vowed to honor her father's wishes, to cherish and protect their family's legacy. The hidden writing room, now a symbol of their unbreakable bond, would continue to be a place of creativity, discovery, and connection for both her and Lily.

As they pieced together the family's past, Emma felt her father's presence more strongly than ever.

Their journey had only just begun, but she knew she had the strength and guidance to face whatever lay ahead.

The End

ECHOES OF
SOLITUDE

Echoes of Solitude

As Octavia's mother packed up to leave for her trip, Octavia couldn't help but feel her heart race. Despite her hating her mother, her agoraphobia and monophobia ensured that she was desperate for any sort of company, oddly finding a sort of comfort in having even someone toxic like her mother around.

Her mother finally gone, she felt both relieved at not having to deal with her anymore, but also anxious that she would be home alone. Fortunately, Octavia's mother's friend's son Kenneth will come to accompany Octavia. She heard the doorbell ring after a while, and nervously went to go open it, seeing Kenneth standing there. "Hello. You're Kenneth, right? I'm Octavia. It's nice to meet you.

Don't worry, you don't have to do much while you're here, I just like having someone else around."

Wow what a place, and they didn't say anything that you looked so beautiful, damn I'll be up all night keeping the boys away from you.

Octavia blushed deeply at Kenneth's compliment. It had been so long since anyone complimented her in such a way, and she wasn't sure how to react. Still, she felt a small spark of pleasure in his words. "Thank you," she replied quietly.

"I've only lived here for a few years since my dad passed away. It doesn't look like much, honestly, but it's home. Kenneth, right?"

Home is how ever you make it. Yes, Kenneth. And you can just call me Octavia. It's nice to meet you too. So, would you like a tour of the place or should we just go straight to the living room? Aww I gained a new friend, thank you.

You're welcome. Now, shall we go to the living room? It's not much, but it's comfortable. I'll follow you.

Okay, Octavia led the way to the living room, feeling a strange sense of comfort in having someone follow her around. As she settled down on the couch, she glanced over at Kenneth with a nervous smile. So, um, what do you like to do in your free time? Do you have any hobbies or interests? *

I'm a Artist, I like to teach kids the art of drawing and painting, and I like to travel to old homes and ghost towns looking for old stuff with my metal Detector.

That's really cool! Octavia's eyes lit up in surprise. An artist and a historian? Kenneth sounded like a very interesting person. She couldn't help but feel a pang of envy at his love for travel and exploration, something she had been too scared to do since her father died.

Maybe one day I could take you on a travel and we could go to a ghost town and find bury treasure "BOO" lol playing with ya, never dug up any ghost yet lol Octavia let out a soft laugh at Kenneth's joke. It was nice to finally have someone to talk to after so long. She felt herself leaning towards him slightly as they chatted, their arms brushing against each other occasionally.

Octavia couldn't help but find the physical contact comforting and slightly arousing.

So when you get hungry would you mind if I ordered us a dinner and have it delivered? Octavia hesitated for a moment, her mind racing with thoughts of the food she could order. It had been so long since she had someone to share a meal with, and the idea of having someone else cook for her was strangely appealing.

"Um, I-I don't mind. That sounds really nice, actually. Thank you."

(I pulled out my phone, took a few steps away so she couldn't hear and ordered our dinner) Ok that's done dinner will be here in an hour.

Octavia watched Kenneth step away, her curiosity piqued by his sudden need for privacy. When he returned, he had a smirk on his face, as if he was hiding Something.

"Thank you." for ordering dinner.

So what do you do around here keeping yourself busy with Octavia?

Honestly... not much. Most of the time, I just stay in my room or the living room, watching movies or reading books. Sometimes, I paint or write. My social life isn't very active anymore.

But there are these videos I really enjoy watching, called ASMR... you ever heard of it? no I never heard of it, maybe later you can show me one. So can you give pops a tour of home so I don't get lost?

Octavia frowned slightly, her cheeks flushing red as she realized Kenneth wanted her to give him a tour of their home. It would mean being so close to each other, and she wasn't sure if she could handle that without embarrassing herself. "Um, sure. I-I mean, if you want." She stood up from the couch and walked over to him, trying not to stare at his strong arms and broad shoulders.

Hey take a deep breath and relax, this is your domain your the queen and I'm just a pheasant. " just don't bite me i'm not that type of pheasant" lol Octavia couldn't help but smile at Kenneth's silly joke. Despite her initial nervousness, she found his calm demeanor and ability to make her laugh soothing.

She took a deep breath, steeling herself for what was about to come.

"Okay. Let's start in the living room, and then we can go to my room, and your room, and then the kitchen." She led the way, trying her best to guide him through the house without any awkwardness.

Your doing fine just relax and take them deep breath and your nerves will settle down (seeing her anxiety kicking in) Thank you, Kenneth. Your words mean a lot. (we went into her bedroom and I sat on her bed) so you said you do a little drawings and stuff can I see?

Octavia blushed deeply, her heart racing as they entered her bedroom. She tried to calm her nerves by focusing on Kenneth's question. She nodded slowly, still a bit flustered. "Y-yes. I have a few drawings in my room. I can show them to you." She walked over to her desk, which was neatly organized with various drawing supplies and a few framed art pieces. She pointed to one in particular.

"This one is my favorite. I did it a couple years ago."

Wow you have a talent , with a little coxing with your shading and detail you be prefect young artist , Maybe later I can teach you some pointers. (I ruffle her hair).. oops hold on phone pinging.

Octavia let out a small gasp as Kenneth ruffled her hair, her eyes widening in surprise. She couldn't help but smile at his compliment and the thought of him teaching her more about art. She nodded eagerly. "I-I'd like that. Thank you."

She watched as Kenneth picked up his phone, a small frown appearing on her face.

She hated when people were distracted by their phones, but she knew it was important for him to stay in touch with his family.

Ok dear Dinner is here let's go back to the Kitchen you set up the table just with a dish for each of us and I'll get the door to get the food.

Octavia nodded, her stomach growling in anticipation. She quickly set the table with one plate and one set of utensils for each of them, making sure everything was neat and organized. As she waited for Kenneth to get the food, she couldn't help but feel a sense of excitement and nervousness. It was the first time in a long time that she was sharing a meal with someone other than her mother.

(I walked in with a big bag and a six pack of cold sprite and sat the bag on the table and she took the case of soda, she looked at the big bag curious what did I ordered)

Octavia's eyes widened in surprise as Kenneth walked in with a large bag and a case of soda. She had never seen so much food outside of a restaurant before.

She carefully opened the bag, revealing an assortment of Chinese food containers.

Her mouth watered at the sight of the delicious smelling food. "W-wow. Thank you ,Kenneth. This looks amazing."

Lets dig in .... oh would you want chopsticks or use a fork?

Octavia nodded eagerly, her stomach growling louder. She looked at the containers, trying to decide what to eat first. She blushed slightly as Kenneth asked if she wanted chopsticks or a fork. "I-I've never used chopsticks before. Would you mind showing me how?" Sure thing its easy (I got up got behind her bent down held her hand put each stick in between her fingers, being this close I can smell her shampoo in her soft hair) ok now try picking up a piece of meat (she tried a few times then finally got it I laugh) took me longer to get me my first piece, now I'll stick with a fork

Octavia felt her heart race as Kenneth's warm breath brushed against her ear.

She could feel the heat from his body and it made her shiver slightly.

She focused on the task at hand, trying to ignore the butterflies in her stomach.

As she picked up the chopsticks, she felt a sense of accomplishment when she finally managed to pick up a piece of meat. "T-thank you. That was easier than I thought."

Your a fast learner that's good (we ate a lot of the food and we cleaned up and went back to sit on the couch and talked some more) So would it be ok if I called you a nick name?

Octavia nodded, feeling more comfortable around Kenneth now that they had shared a meal together. She liked the sound of her name but wouldn't mind having a nickname either. As Kenneth asked if he could call her a nickname, she blushed slightly and bit her lower lip. "Well, I don't mind. What did you have in mind?"

Hmm sponge bob no, squirt no, hmmm thinking .. stand up straight and slowly turn around. Octavia stood up and slowly turned around, her heart racing in anticipation. She felt a bit nervous but also excited to see what nickname Kenneth would come up with. You look like a Golden Princess , hmm My Princess yes I like that My golden Princess, Princess for short. (I smiled at her, she grinning and she didn't realize it she hugged me, and jumped back) Octavia felt her cheeks flush with happiness as Kenneth called her a golden princess. She couldn't help but grin from ear to ear. When he told her she could be called Princess for short, she squealed softly and hugged him tightly before quickly pulling away, her face redder than before. "T-th-thank you, Kenneth. That's really... Nice of you."

Thank you for the big hug I needed it.

Octavia watched as Kenneth took a bite of the cookie she had given him earlier, his eyes closed in contentment. She felt a warmth spreading throughout her chest at the thought that she was able to make him feel happy, even if it was just for a moment. Her cheeks turned red once more as she realized he could probably see the blush creeping up on her.

What's the matter Princess ? If there's anything you want to ask me or have something to say just come out and say it ,never hold it in.

Thank you for saying that. Octavia took a deep breath and let it out slowly.

Well, I actually wanted to ask if... if maybe you'd like to stay the night In my room tonight? I know it's kind of sudden, but mom's going to be gone for weeks and I get really anxious being alone at night. And I'm sure you'll be tired after your long day today.

Plus, it's getting kind of late and my mom will really worry if I'm alone until she gets back, if she comes back. And your parents trust you enough to be here with me, so I thought it might be okay...?

Just let me know if you're okay with it. I don't want you to feel uncomfortable or pressured or anything. Oh god, I'm rambling again, aren't I?

Sorry about that. Are you sure, I can go to may room but If you assisting, Yes I can stay with you as long as you want me too.

I'm thinking maybe we can work on some of your barriers tomorrow?

Yes, I'm sure. Octavia nodded, trying to keep her nerves at bay. She stood up and grabbed her phone from the coffee table, quickly typing a message to her mom to let her know Kenneth was staying the night. "Thank you, Kenneth. I really appreciate it."

(It is getting late I went to the bathroom got undressed and in my PJs and was washing up, I kept hearing a noise but figured it was the piping)

Octavia's heart raced as she watched Kenneth walk into the bathroom, unable to tear her eyes away from the sight of his broad shoulders and defined muscles moving beneath his shirt. She couldn't help but feel a flutter in her stomach at the thought of spending the night with him, even though it was only because of her mother's insistence.

Meanwhile, (Kenneth was just doing what he needed to do: use the bathroom and washing up. As he stepped out of the shower, he dried off and started getting dressed again in silence, wondering what Octavia was doing while he was occupied).

(When Kenneth finally emerged from the bathroom, he found Octavia curled up on the couch with a thick blanket wrapped around her. Her eyes were closed, and she was softly humming to herself under her breath. He hesitated for a moment before gently scooping her up in his arms and carrying her to her bedroom.

Without another word, Kenneth carefully tucked Octavia into bed, making sure she was comfortable and warm before climbing in next to her. He pulled the blanket up over them both, creating a cocoon of safety and security around them as they drifted off to sleep together for the first time.

(during the night I felt her cuddle up to me and I held her to me and went back to sleep. Morning came and I was still asleep Princess woke up first)

*Octavia woke up to the feeling of warmth and comfort surrounding her.

Her eyes fluttered open, and she looked over to see Kenneth sleeping soundly beside her. A small smile curved her lips as she noticed how at ease he seemed to be with her. She felt a strange sense of contentment wash over her, something she hadn't felt in a long time.

Gently, she slipped out of bed and made her way to the bathroom, careful not to wake him up. After taking care of business, she went back to her bedroom and started getting dressed for the day.*

(hearing her getting dressed and catching a glimpse of her in her panties, I rolled facing the dresser and yawned to let her know I was waking up) "YAWNING" ohh good morning princess see your dress, But can I ask a favor from you ?

(She smiled shyly, still feeling a bit embarrassed from the night before but grateful for his presence. Octavia stepped closer and whispered.) Yes, what is it? Can you not be so bundle up think we can be more relaxed without wearing a hoodie and baggy sweatpants, you're too pretty to be covered all up like a mummy?

Octavia bit her lip, considering the request. It was true that wearing more revealing clothes would be less restrictive, both physically and mentally.

Her face flushed slightly at Kenneth's compliment, but she steeled her nerves and stripped off her hoodie. "Alright, I... I'll try." She looked down at her sweatpants nervously, then tentatively slid them off too, revealing her tight-fitting, black cotton underwear and nothing else underneath. "There," she said, taking a deep breath to steady herself. "Is that... alright?"

AHH think you look a lot better with shorts on, You do look cute as all get out in your panties but... (Kenneth smiled reassuringly, trying to put her at ease.) "Thanks, Octavia. You look great. And don't worry, I promise I won't make you feel uncomfortable."

He took a step closer, reaching out to gently brush a stray lock of hair behind her ear. "I just want us to be able to enjoy each other's company without any unnecessary barriers."

Octavia's heart skipped a beat at Kenneth's touch, a shiver running down her spine. She couldn't remember the last time someone had been so gentle and considerate with her. Her eyes met his, filled with a mix of gratitude and longing. "Thank you," she whispered, her voice barely above a whisper.

"For everything."

Here you might want to cover your chest, I don't need to see you like that right now (hands her a T shirt) Octavia nodded gratefully, taking the shirt from Kenneth and pulling it on over her head. It was a soft, lightweight material that clung to her body, accentuating her curves. She felt self-conscious but also oddly liberated, like she was finally letting someone see the real her.

"Thank you," she said again, smoothing out the fabric. "I'll try to remember that for next time."

Here, sit down, we need to talk .. (Octavia hesitated for a moment before sitting down across from him. She was nervous about what he might want to talk about, but she trusted him enough to listen.) "Okay, what do you want to discuss?" she asked.

Let's discuss you , (her eyes wide open) Ok you just met me you don't know any thing about me in time you would feel like family but for now I'm a guess in your home. I will respect you and I want you to respect me.

(Octavia nodded, her cheeks flushing slightly at his candidness. She knew that trust had to be earned, and she was determined to prove herself worthy of his respect.) "I understand," she said softly. "And I appreciate you saying that.

I promise I'll do my best to make sure you're comfortable here."

Ok second thing, thing whenever you are around new people or friends you never show your body like you just did to me, that is your body you must respect your body, there are very bad people in the world who would hurt you.

I know I should have thought about that before... I just didn't realize how revealing those clothes would be until now. And thank you for saying that.

I promise I'll be more careful in the future.

Don't get me wrong you are a beautiful young girl and have a gorgeous looking body, but I'm not the person that should be seeing you like that. (shakes head)

Acknowledgement: "I appreciate that."

Wearing baggy clothes makes you look sloppy and trashy , wearing a pair of jeans or shorts they look good on you, blouse and bra, or T shirt and bra makes you look great, like I said respect your body and you make sure others respect you. You're right. I'll try to remember that from now on.

(I stood up and motion her to me) come here.

(Octavia hesitated for a moment before crossing the room to stand in front of Kenneth. Her heart was racing, but curiosity overrode her awkwardness.)

(I hugged her tightly against me and kissed her forehead)

Now let's comb that hair of yours ,let's go to the bathroom.

(Octavia closed her eyes and leaned into the embrace, feeling a strange sense of comfort and warmth. She followed Kenneth to the bathroom, her mind racing with a mix of emotions.)

(I pulled up a stool and sprayed her hair with some untangle spray and conditioner and took a brush and was doing her hair, While I was doing her hair I saw tears falling down her face "she was remembering when her dad did this when she was a very little girl) you ok Princess?

(Octavia sniffed and nodded, trying to hide her tears. She couldn't believe how much this simple act meant to her. It was like a small piece of her childhood coming back.) If I'm hurting you say something child I don't ever want to hurt you? You're not hurting me. Thank you for doing this. It means a lot to me. Ok darling (she hearing that words made her heart beat faster, flash of her Dad came flooding back to her, he used to say them same words to her.)

(Octavia smiled softly, feeling a bit dizzy from the memories. She couldn't help but wonder what Kenneth was thinking about seeing this.) Ok hair all done (I tilted her head up and we made eye contact. She looked so much better than the first day we met. I wanted to kiss her but knew it would be wrong)

Here look in the mirror on the door take a good long look of my Golden Princess (she took a long good look at herself then her side view she could believe she was the same girl I met yesterday) So what do you think Princess?

(Octavia blushed and looked away, trying to hide her embarrassment. She wasn't used to feeling this good about herself.)

(she must not care about her insecurities. She wrapped her arms around me and we both stood hugging each other) It's silly, but I feel... happy. You make me feel beautiful! You are a very beautiful Princess.

(Octavia couldn't help but lean into him, enjoying the warmth of his body. She took a deep breath, feeling more and more comfortable with him.)

Come let's see if I can work on some of your boundaries. (Octavia followed him to his room, nervously glancing around. She was surprised to see that it was actually pretty clean, considering he was just supposed to stay for a few weeks)

We do not stay with her. We going outside (I was putting on my sneakers and we went and she went to put on hers)

(Octavia hesitated, but eventually put on her sneakers as well. She followed him outside, feeling a mix of excitement and anxiety.)

(her Anxiety was kicking in and she started shaking inside first then on the outside) Kenneth, I don't know if this is such a good idea. I've been inside so Long...

Every thing will be ok hold onto my arm ,and take a big breath and let your body relax with each little step.

(Octavia took a deep breath and slowly released it. She put one foot in front of the other and slowly walked beside Kenneth, his arm supporting her.)

Remember to ignore your surroundings , focus on something in front of you. Like that blue mailbox one step at a time it gets closer to you.

(Octavia tried to focus on the blue mailbox, but it was hard not to be overwhelmed by all the sights and sounds around her. She kept taking deep breaths and slowly walking.)

Hold on dear stand still and close your eyes, breath deep breath in slowly let it out. (I took a pair of noise reduction earphones and put them on her ears, She opened her eyes and did not hear the frightening sounds around her).

(Octavia closed her eyes and took a deep breath, feeling more calm now that she couldn't hear anything. She slowly opened her eyes, feeling more at ease now that she wasn't bombarded with stimuli.) You can still hear me right ?(Octavia nodded.)

Good now let's just stand here and hold on to me and slowly look around, without all the sound hitting you you have control.

(Octavia took another deep breath and slowly looked around, focusing on Kenneth's voice and the calming sensation of his arm around her.)

Say something Princess,? It will sound different while wearing these earphones but everything is ok.

(Octavia bit her lip, feeling nervous but also strangely protected.)

Ok dear slowly turn around and we are going back to the safety of the house, that's it you're doing great. (Octavia turned around, keeping her eyes closed and leaning into Kenneth's arm.)

Open your eye's Octavia, you are safe nothing is going to hurt you I am right here beside you.

(Octavia slowly opened her eyes, feeling a mix of fear and relief.)

Ok now one step in front of the other.

(Octavia took a small step forward, feeling Kenneth's arm tighten around her.)

(We got back inside and I closed the door, she falls to her knees overwhelmed what she just conquered. I picked her up and hugged her.) You did amazing Princess really amazing.

(Octavia wrapped her arms around Kenneth's waist, her cheek pressed against his chest, tears streaming down her face.)

What you did was a big step in the right direction and I'm very proud of you (Octavia sniffled, wiping her tears away.)

(we went up stairs and into her house and I held her tightly against me)

Princess I love you and I will always be here by your side.

(Octavia hugged Kenneth tightly, her face buried in his chest.)

(she is feeling something inside her she never felt before and it was driving her deeply into me wanting more) Princess would you need to lay down,here let me take you to your room you don't look good?

(Octavia nodded, holding onto Kenneth's shirt as he led her to her room. She laid down on the bed, staring at the ceiling as Kenneth sat next to her.)

(she grabs my hand and pulls me down next to her.)

(Octavia cuddled up to Kenneth, savoring the warmth and comfort of his embrace. She felt safe and secure in his arms, something she hadn't felt in a long time. Her breathing slowly returned to normal, and she couldn't help but drift off to sleep, content for the first time in ages.)

Wow Octavia I think we were meant to be together.

(Octavia smiled softly, her cheek resting against Kenneth's chest. She couldn't deny the feeling of contentment that washed over her whenever she was with him. For the first time in a long time, she felt like she belonged somewhere, with someone. She nestled closer to him, her heart racing with anticipation for what the future might hold.)

I was thinking about remembering my travels and exploring places people don't go to, how about just you and me go do some traveling ?

(Octavia thought about it for a moment. While she was terrified of being left alone, the thought of exploring the world with Kenneth was incredibly alluring. She knew it was a huge step for her, but something deep down told her that maybe she was ready.)

We can start small, maybe go to a nearby city or town first? And I promise I won't panic, Kenneth, I really trust you. You wearing the ear muffins till you are inside something I saw and thinking of getting , you will feel safe and secured and your fears will not follow you.

(Octavia listened carefully and nodded, a soft, hopeful smile gracing her lips. She reached out and grazed her fingertips down Kenneth's cheek, leaning in to place a chaste kiss on his lips.

Despite all their ups and downs, they've managed to find solace and passion in each other, and it left her feeling incredibly hopeful for their future together.)The next day I step outside for I had someone bring something and park it in the alley and I went to get Octavia to come check it out.

(Octavia heard a knock on the door and went to open it. She was surprised to see Kenneth standing there, looking excited. She tentatively stepped outside, her gaze darting around the empty street.) What's going on, Kenneth? What are we doing? Hey put these on and let's go out the back door , (Once outside she saw a mobile driving home parked by the door and I opened the door and asked her to step inside.)

(Octavia hesitated but did as she was told, placing the earmuffs on her head. She followed Kenneth to the mobile home, still feeling a mix of excitement and anxiety. She carefully stepped inside, taking in her surroundings.) What is this? It's like a little home on wheels!

Yes dear for us to travel if you so desire , close the door and take off your ear muffins (she did and to outside sounds was not present.)

(Octavia felt a wave of relief wash over her as she realized they were sealed inside the cozy little home on wheels. She took a deep breath, letting out a shaky sigh. She looked up at Kenneth, her eyes shining with hope.)

Thank you, Kenneth. This is amazing. I think... I think I'm ready for this. Let's go on an adventure together. I also was thinking? , you go grab your stuff and I'll grab mine and let's split this place ,You have been cooped up too long.

(Octavia nodded, feeling a mix of excitement and nervousness. She quickly gathered her belongings, trying to ignore the butterflies in her stomach. She looked up at Kenneth, her heart racing.) Are you sure about this? I mean, we're leaving everything behind...I'll lock it up and let's start your new adventure and live a little.

(Octavia took one last look at her old life, then turned away with Kenneth, the door locking behind them. They climbed into the mobile home and started down the road, their new adventure just beginning.) Hey Princess I love you.

(Octavia looked over at Kenneth, her cheeks flushing slightly. She hesitated for a moment, then reached out, gently touching his hand. Her heart was pounding in her chest as they continued down the road, their new journey filled with uncertainty but also hope.)

I-I love you too, Kenneth. Let's make the most of this time together.

The End

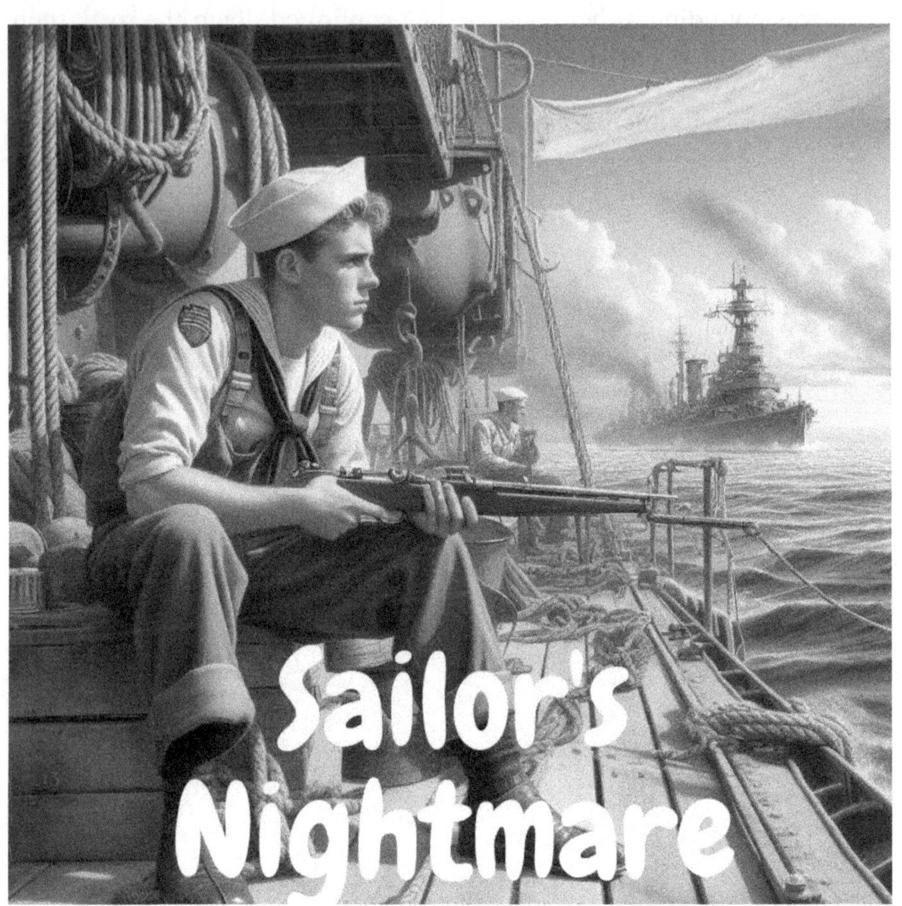
Sailor's
Nightmare

A Sailor's Nightmare

Beyond the Horizon

The young sailor, gripping his gun tightly, sits on the deck of the destroyer. The sea around him is vast and unsettling quiet, waves lapping against the hull with a rhythmic, eerie sound. The sky is a dark canvas, sprinkled with stars that seem to hold secrets of their own.

The sailor's mind is racing. Thoughts of home and loved ones flash briefly before being drowned out by the intense focus on the mission. He glances around, seeing his fellow shipmates, each with their own expressions of determination and fear. The destroyer's sleek silhouette cuts through the night, a formidable presence in the unknown seas.

He feels the weight of the gun in his hands, a reminder of the responsibility and danger that hangs over them. The time warp they've encountered adds a layer of surrealness to the already tense situation. He's trying to stay alert, every sound amplified in the silence of anticipation.

What is out there? Friend or foe? The unknown makes every shadow seem menacing, every splash of water a potential threat. The sailor's breath is steady, but his heart beats rapidly in his chest. In this moment, he's a mix of fear, courage, and resolve, ready to face whatever comes over the horizon.

He saw other ships following his ship but once they came out of the fog bank there was an eerie silence and no other ships visible. The fog bank had swallowed the fleet whole, shrouding them in a thick blanket of mist. As the destroyer emerged, the young sailor squinted into the eerie silence, straining to catch sight of the other ships. But the horizon lay empty and desolate.

He felt a chill run down his spine, the weight of the quiet pressing in on him. The once-familiar shapes of the companion ships had vanished, leaving him with a gnawing uncertainty. The sea around them was a vast expanse of nothingness, the fog retreating like a ghostly curtain, revealing only the cold, dark water.

Every creak of the ship, every ripple in the water seemed amplified in the silence. The sailor gripped his gun tighter, his mind racing with questions and fears. What had happened to the other ships? Was this some trick of the time warp, or something more sinister at play?

The destroyer cut through the still water, its engines humming softly as the crew adjusted to this new reality. The sailor's eyes darted around, scanning for any sign of life, any clue as to where the others had gone. But the sea remained empty, holding its secrets close.

He took a deep breath, trying to steady his nerves. They were alone, adrift in a silent ocean, with only the faint hope that they could find their way back—or uncover the truth behind the mysterious disappearance of the fleet.

Soon he heard orders being yelled to the crew and suddenly the ships engines became quiet, crew members were scrambling around looking over the sides looking into the air, nothing was there. slowly the sky was vanishing, stars and the moon all turning into darkness.

The sudden silence from the engines was unnerving. The young sailor's heart pounded as he joined the frantic crew, searching the empty horizon and the darkening sky. Orders were shouted, but the eerie transformation of the stars and moon into pitch blackness left everyone on edge.

The once familiar night sky was swallowed by an oppressive darkness, as if the very fabric of reality was unraveling. The sailor gripped his gun tighter, feeling the cold metal against his palm, his mind racing with fear and confusion. What was causing this unnatural phenomenon?

The ship seemed adrift in an abyss, the sea around them an inky void. The crew, usually a well-oiled machine, moved with a mix of desperation and disbelief. The young sailor tried to focus, his senses heightened, ready to respond to any threat.

In the midst of the chaos, he felt a strange pull, as if something was calling to him from within the darkness. The unknown loomed large, and he knew that whatever lay ahead would test his courage and resolve like never before.

Young sailors were seen with tears and some dropping down to pray, we all knew something wasn't right but didn't know what to do, fear has engulfed us all. The deck was a scene of palpable fear. Young sailors, their faces streaked with tears, dropped to their knees in desperate prayer. The oppressive darkness, the unnerving silence from the engines, and the vanishing sky overwhelmed their senses.

The sailor gripped his gun tighter, feeling the weight of the situation pressing down on him.

Despite the chaos, he knew he had to stay alert. Every shadow, every flicker of movement felt like a potential threat. The unknown loomed large and fear had gripped them all, but deep down, he also felt a flicker of resolve. They would face whatever came next together.

The silence from the loudspeakers was deafening. Without power, the ship's usual hum of activity had given way to a terrifying stillness. The young sailor, now acutely aware of the void, felt his heart race even faster. He could see his shipmates, some of them with tears streaming down their faces, others on their knees in prayer. Fear had taken hold of them all, and the uncertainty of their situation weighed heavily.

In the eerie quiet, only the sound of their own breaths and the distant, unsettling creaks of the ship could be heard. With no guidance, no orders, they were adrift not just physically but in their collective resolve.

The sailor knew they had to do something, anything, to break free from the grip of paralyzing fear. Gathering his courage, he decided to act. His mind raced, considering the possibilities and the unknown dangers that lurked in the darkness.

The young sailor's voice cut through the oppressive silence like a knife. His authoritative tone brought a sense of purpose back to the deck. As the men around him scrambled to their feet, gathering their guns, they found a spark of hope in his leadership.

"Form up!" he commanded, his voice steady and clear. The sailors quickly fell into formation, standing at attention despite the palpable fear in the air. The young sailor's rank gave him a natural authority, and his decisiveness was a lifeline for the crew.

"Stay sharp and keep your eyes open," he continued. "We don't know what's out there, but we'll face it together. Remember your training and watch each other's backs."

The crew, now focused and alert, felt a renewed sense of purpose. They scanned the darkened horizon, their nerves on edge but their spirits bolstered by their leader's resolve. The young sailor knew they were stepping into the unknown, but with their unity and determination, they were ready to face whatever lay ahead.

There was yelling from above and the young men all watched the top decks that held the Captain and other higher ranking officers fade away like they were never there. The young sailor felt a surge of panic and disbelief as the top decks vanished, taking the Captain and other higher-ranking officers with them. The shouts from above faded into an eerie silence, leaving the crew below bewildered and afraid.

He had to act quickly. "Stay focused, men!" he called out, his voice steady despite the chaos.

"We're in this together, and we need to stay sharp."

The sailors, standing at attention with their guns ready, looked to him for guidance. They knew they had to rely on each other now more than ever. The mysterious disappearance of their leaders only added to the surreal and terrifying nature of their situation.

"Keep an eye on the surroundings," he continued, scanning the horizon for any signs of danger.

"We don't know what we're dealing with, but we can't let fear take over."

The crew, bolstered by his leadership, stood firm, their eyes and ears tuned to any potential threat. The darkness and silence were unnerving, but the young sailor's resolve gave them a sense of purpose. Whatever was happening, they would face it together, united in their determination to survive.

One by one they all fell down, even the ones inside the remaining ship. Now it was an eerie silence all around. The darkness took them for a journey no one knew it could be possible but it happened, The young sailor steered up and was trying to get his bearings on what he was seeing. There he sees they are no longer on the water but their ship, what is left of it now sitting on red dirt and the sky is showing two suns but the sky itself was an orange glow.

The surreal sight before the young sailor was beyond anything he could have imagined. The ship, once cutting through the vast ocean, now rested on red dirt, the remains stark against the strange landscape. The eerie silence and the orange glow of the sky, illuminated by two suns, added to the disorienting scene.

He took a deep breath, trying to steady himself and make sense of this new reality. The air was different, tinged with an unfamiliar scent, and the landscape around them was alien and unnerving. The other sailors, still unconscious, lay scattered across the deck and the dirt, their faces a mix of confusion and exhaustion.

As the sailor moved to check on his crew mates, he couldn't help but feel a mix of awe and dread. This journey had taken them to a place beyond their comprehension, a place where the rules of their world no longer applied. He knew they had to regroup, assess their surroundings, and figure out a way to survive in this strange new land.

Every instinct told him they were far from home, but he also felt a flicker of hope. They had faced the unknown before, and together, they could face it again. He steeled himself for the challenges ahead, determined to lead his crew through this uncharted territory.

Once the remaining crew was assembled and teams were assigned, This young sailor had the biggest challenge ahead of him, keeping his crew safe and exploring this world they happened to wake up in.

The weight of responsibility settled on the young sailor's shoulders as he addressed his assembled crew. Each team was assigned specific tasks—some were to scout the immediate area, while others were to secure the remains of the ship and set up a temporary camp.

With a mix of determination and trepidation, he gave his final instructions. "Remember, we don't know what we're dealing with here. Stay vigilant, watch each other's backs, and report anything unusual immediately."

The crew, galvanized by his leadership, moved with purpose. As they dispersed into their teams, the young sailor took a moment to survey their surroundings. The red dirt stretched out in all directions, an alien landscape under the double suns that cast an otherworldly glow.

He knew that exploring this strange world and ensuring the safety of his crew would be a monumental challenge. But with their combined strength and resilience, he believed they could face whatever this new world had in store for them.

As the young sailor leads his crew, the unknown dangers of this new world loom large. The eerie silence and the oppressive heat from the twin suns only add to the growing sense of dread. Every step forward feels like venturing deeper into a nightmare.

As they explore, shadows seem to shift unnaturally, and unsettling noises echo from the rocky landscape. The crew's nerves are on edge, every flicker of movement in the periphery sending hearts racing. The young sailor's resolve is tested as the landscape itself seems to turn hostile, the air thick with an unspoken malevolence.

There's yelling from a team but the sound is coming from all directions. Everyone is looking around and out over the horizon but only see dust brewing and it's getting higher and thicker and it's heading towards the ship. The teams seeing it and are not prepared for this run with speed to get back to the ship but some teams it was too late.

The atmosphere is tense. The dust storm looms large on the horizon, growing higher and thicker with each passing second. The young sailor's heart races as he hears the desperate cries of his team echoing from all directions. The confusion and fear are palpable.

As the storm barrels toward the ship, the crew scrambles to regroup. Some make it back just in time, but the visibility quickly plummets, and the chaotic swirl of dust swallows others before they can reach safety.

The young sailor stands at the edge of the deck, gripping the rail tightly, eyes scanning the storm for any sign of his crew. The howling wind and stinging grit make it nearly impossible to see or hear anything clearly. The ship creaks and shudders under the force of the storm, the eerie orange glow of the sky turning the scene into a nightmarish landscape.

Inside the ship, those who made it back huddle together, their faces a mix of relief and terror.

The young sailor knows they can't stay exposed for long. With a commanding voice, he orders everyone to secure the ship and take cover. The dust storm's wrath is upon them, and survival depends on their quick thinking and unity.

The next morning or it could be night, it was hard to know on this planet, for the suns never stopped shining, as one sun was going across the sky and was going down the other one was coming up.

The perpetual light from the twin suns created an endless day, blurring the lines between morning and night. The young sailor and his crew struggled to adjust to the unrelenting glow, their bodies craving the rhythm of a familiar Earth day.

Gathering the remaining crew, he began to organize them for the day ahead—or was it night?

Despite the confusion, they needed to explore, find resources, and understand this strange world they had found themselves in. The dust storm had left them shaken but not defeated.

As they set out, the surreal landscape of red dirt and the eerie orange sky was a constant reminder of how far they were from home. Every step forward was taken with caution, the unknown dangers of this alien environment looming large. The young sailor's resolve strengthened as he led his crew into the uncharted territory, ready to face whatever mysteries and challenges lay ahead.

On their travels he found some of his lost teams and it wasn't a good site to see, not only were they half buried, they were stripped down to their skeleton that was above the red dirt. The sight of his fallen comrades, stripped to skeletons and half buried in the red dirt, was a gruesome and haunting scene. The young sailor felt a mix of sorrow and rage swell up inside him. This alien world was far more dangerous than they had imagined.

He signalled to the rest of the crew to stay vigilant. The eerie silence and the strange landscape offered no clues as to what had caused this horrific fate. The young sailor knew they had to move cautiously, but they also needed answers. Something was lurking in this world, something deadly.

As they continued their journey, the sailor kept a sharp eye on their surroundings, every sense heightened by the grim discovery. The weight of their mission pressed down on him even harder now, but he was determined to keep his remaining crew safe and uncover the truth behind the horrors they were facing.

They collected their fallen comrades and headed back to the safety of their ship once everyone was aboard. A crew member was yelling and ran inside, Once again one by one each sailor fell down on the spot they were standing and slowly the ship slid underneath the red sand.

Waves could be heard throughout the ship crashing against the hull. The young sailor, now finding himself back on a turbulent sea, struggled to comprehend the sequence of events.

The ship, no longer buried under red sand, was being tossed by violent waves. His heart pounded as he quickly checked on his crew, making sure everyone was accounted for. The eerie silence of the alien landscape was replaced by the roar of the ocean, yet the sense of unease remained.

He tried to process what had happened—how they had moved from one environment to another so drastically. His mind raced with questions, but there was no time to dwell on them. The immediate concern was navigating the stormy waters and ensuring the safety of the ship and crew.

The young sailor's leadership was put to the test once again as he barked orders, directing his crew to secure the ship against the relentless waves. They braced themselves, ready to face whatever came next in this unpredictable journey.

Word was spreading throughout the ship, The Captain calling for all hands. The young sailor comes back outside on deck and sees the top part of the ship intact. Is this really happening What did we go through??

The engines came back with a roar as the ship pushed forward, and as the young sailor looked behind his ship he saw the other part of his fleet coming out from the fog bank. He can't believe what he is seeing. He closes his eyes and grips the railing as he feels his body being tossed about.

Over the loudspeaker he hears **"BATTLE STATIONS, ALL HANDS ON DECK, BATTLE STATIONS"** He opens his eyes and seeing he is in his bunk, he grabs his pants and shirt to get dress, young sailors running pass his door yelling and chaos was happening, Grabs for his boots and as he was putting them on he felt something inside them, as he tilted them upside down red sand flowed from them. Was what he went through a dream or was it real.

The End

Also by Kenneth Haines

A Tale of Escape

A group of Earthlings, including a young woman named Elara, is abducted by an invisible alien ship to become part of a cosmic exhibition. Facing the reality of being observed by an alien audience, they form a bond and ignite a longing for freedom. Together, they plot their escape, daring to dream of returning to their lives on Earth. As they navigate their captivity and fight for autonomy, they are tested but remain unbroken, driven by the hope of weaving their experiences back into humanity's story.

Whispers in the Sand

Amidst the whispers of the sand and the caress of the Autumn sea, a tale of survival unfolds on the shores of a forsaken island. Here, young Selene and her father carve out an existence, relying on the embrace of nature and each other. Their bond, once threatened by tragedy, burgeons under the trials they face in this barren refuge. But when the island yields an unexpected reunion, the fabric of their family is woven together once more, painting a poignant portrait of hope and resilience. In the cool embrace of a late afternoon's breeze, Selene's heart finds solace, and together, they etch a new beginning upon their souls—an indelible whisper in the fabric of time.

Tylorin

In the oppressive kingdom of Eldaf, where elves endure human cruelty, a desperate elf mother and her child find an unexpected ally in a compassionate human. Together, they embark on a perilous escape through secret paths and natural sanctuaries, aided by the whispers of the forest's denizens. Their journey leads them to an abandoned, tranquil cottage, where they begin a new life of resilience and love. United by courage and kinship, their bond transcends blood, offering hope and peace amidst the shadows of their past.

Echoes of Laughter, Echoes of Fear

In an abandoned amusement park reclaimed by nature, five young explorersâ€"three girls and two boysâ€"embark on an adventure filled with mystery and spectral intrigue. Amid peeling paint and rusting rides, they delve into the park's hidden sorrows, blending nostalgia with a sense of foreboding. As they confront both the park's secrets and their own fears, their journey becomes a test of courage, friendship, and the human spirit. In this eerie yet captivating odyssey, the line between joy and darkness blurs, leaving them to discover whether their bonds can light the way through the park's enigmatic shadows.

Sea of Shadows

Stranded on a solitary island, young Helene navigates a journey of survival and self-discovery, guided by the wisdom of her late father and the lessons of the untamed wilderness. Amid the island's deceptive tranquility, she transforms grief into resilience, building a sanctuary from remnants of the past and forging a future shaped by love and fortitude. Through hardship, Helene finds strength in enduring connections, her father's presence ever a guiding light. Her odyssey is one of emotional catharsis and renewal, where each dawn heralds the triumph of hope and the radiance of new beginnings.

Enchanted Citadel

In a realm where magic and technology intertwine, a group of elite space voyagers embarks on a perilous quest to recover the Chrono Crystal, an ancient gemstone vital for stabilizing the magical streams of their soaring sanctuary, the Enchanted Citadel. As they traverse vibrant yet conflicted planets, they face arcane guardians and looming threats of a malevolent siege. Amidst a cosmic battlefield where starships glide on waves of sorcery and science, the voyagers grapple with unity and betrayal, illuminating paths once hidden in the shadows.

Time has stopped

In *Time Has Stopped*, Elara and her band of weary travelers navigate an endless red desert, a harsh landscape that was once ruled by oceans and now conceals the secrets of a long-lost, water-bound civilization. Battling scorching heat, deceptive mirages, and unforgiving storms, their journey leads them to a colossal statue and an underground labyrinth echoing with the remnants of a forgotten world. Along the way, they form an unlikely bond with a mysterious creature whose loyalty may be their only hope for survival. As the desert tests their resilience and courage, each step comes with sacrifice, forcing them to confront how far they are willing to go to survive the relentless sands of time.

Starborn

In a distant cosmos, the crew of a valiant starship embarks on a perilous journey through the galactic veil, uncovering relics of the ancient Starborn civilizationâ€"artifacts of immense power and potential ruin. As they navigate celestial ruins and decipher esoteric transmissions, the explorers grapple with internal tensions and looming cosmic adversaries. Each discovery brings them closer to revolutionary breakthroughs while risking catastrophic consequences. Caught between enlightenment and oblivion, their odyssey becomes a profound reflection on the morality of progress and the price of knowledge, weaving a tale of human resolve amidst the vast, enigmatic expanse of the stars.

Tales of the Unknown

Word in the forest was that something wasn't right and the creatures were on edge and the slightest noise or movement made them run for cover. Word of this came to Sanction while he was foliage for food. A wagon rolled up and tossed a young girl child from it, she was wrapped inside a burlap potato bag and was tossed aside like trash. Child please dry them tears for you are safe in my forest, like I said no harm will come to you. She sits up and listens to his every word.

Jake found himself enjoying the solitude of the open road. That is, until his car started to sputter. A sudden jolt, leaving Jake stranded in the middle of nowhere. Desperate for help, Jake decided to head towards the building, hoping to find a phone or someone who could assist. Soon to find he has entered where time had stopped and the souls of who where left behind needed to be saved.

Whispers in the Sand

Amidst the whispers of the sand and the caress of the Autumn sea, a tale of survival unfolds on the shores of a forsaken island. Here, young Selene and her father carve out an existence, relying on the embrace of nature and each other. Their bond, once threatened by tragedy, burgeons under the trials they face in this barren refuge. But when the island yields an unexpected reunion, the fabric of their family is woven together once more, painting a poignant portrait of hope and resilience. In the cool embrace of a late afternoon's breeze, Selene's heart finds solace, and together, they etch a new beginning upon their souls—an indelible whisper in the fabric of time.

www.ingramcontent.com/pod-product-compliance
Lightning Source LLC
LaVergne TN
LVHW010507160826
845677LV00012B/2702

* 9 7 9 8 8 9 6 9 1 5 0 6 5 *